But of Course

But of Course

Tatyana Dickinson

But of Course
Copyright © 2020 by Tatyana Dickinson

Library of Congress Control Number: 2020900943
ISBN-13:   Paperback: 978-1-64749-046-1
            ePub: 978-1-64749-047-8

Detective

All rights reserved. No part of this publication may be reproduced, distributed, or transmitted in any form or by any means, including photocopying, recording, or other electronic or mechanical methods, without the prior written permission of the publisher or author, except in the case of brief quotations embodied in critical reviews and certain other noncommercial uses permitted by copyright law.

Although every precaution has been taken to verify the accuracy of the information contained herein, the author and publisher assume no responsibility for any errors or omissions. No liability is assumed for damages that may result from the use of information contained within.

Printed in the United States of America

GoToPublish LLC
1-888-337-1724
www.gotopublish.com
info@gotopublish.com

CONTENTS

Introduction xi
Acknowledgments xiii
Prologue xv
Chapter 1 1
Chapter 2 5
Chapter 3 11
Chapter 4 15
Chapter 5 17
Chapter 6 19
Chapter 7 23
Chapter 8 27
Chapter 9 31
Chapter 10 35
Chapter 11 37
Chapter 12 39
Chapter 13 41
Chapter 14 45
Chapter 15 47
Chapter 16 51
Chapter 17 55

Chapter 18 59
Chapter 19 61
Chapter 20 63
Chapter 21 67
Chapter 22 71
Chapter 23 75
Chapter 24 77
Chapter 25 79
Chapter 26 83
Chapter 27 87
Chapter 28 91
Chapter 29 95
Chapter 30 99
Chapter 31 103
Chapter 32 105
Chapter 33 107
Chapter 34 111
Chapter 35 115
Chapter 36 119
Chapter 37 121
Chapter 38 125

Dave, I'm glad you're doing what you're doing right now, and I hope we will beat all amputations and surgery scars! I also hope we will be together for many more years! Keep on doing it!

Love,

Tanya

They say life is like a train.

Some people hop on any stops or hop off, whether they want to or not.

Some people make a difference in your life; some are gone without you even noticing. In the meantime, we all enjoy good conversations with fellow passengers and learn from each other.

I'm glad you are the passenger on my train. Enjoy the ride!

Cheers,

Tatyana Dickinson

INTRODUCTION

I was born in Kiev, Ukraine (back then it was USSR). Actually, I was born in a plane from Moscow to Kiev, and I have a medal for it!

I moved to the United States back in 1995 and got married in fifteen days to my husband, Dave. We are still together twenty-six years later, and he still fascinates me with his knowledge and experience.

I started the first book years ago, but after he got sick and while taking him from one hospital to another, I decided to do something with my off-work time. I finished and published the first book, *Good Morning after Supper*. This is the second book, and I hope you will enjoy it as much as the first one.

> Do what you can, with what you have, where you are.
> —Theodore Roosevelt

ACKNOWLEDGMENTS

I would like to express a deep gratitude to my husband, Dave, for inspiration and encouragement to share what was going on years ago in USSR. It's not all that different now between the US and Russia. Between the two most powerful countries, there always will be competiveness and "muscle flexing" in front of one and the other. I have been on both sides and heard both sides. I'm proud of what I could accomplish with my true good friends Jojo, Rency, Maknata, Fred, and my husband. Thank you for your motivation and feedback on my books!

PROLOGUE

I was working the night shift from 1500 to 2300 in one of our local nursing homes as a CNA (certified nurse assistant). This job was going under my skin very fast, and I had no idea if I was built strong enough to pull it off.

But of course, I rarely underestimate my skills or knowledge, so I guess I can do this for another week or so.

It's funny how we grow up with parents that expect you to be much better than themselves. In my old country, USSR, they push their kids and themselves because they did not get the break in any aspect of their life.

I'm very surprised to find myself worrying about how to clean the resident's behind and to put the wipes in the different bag as the cleaning towels.

I came to US twenty-six years ago without any dream or desire to live in a little town, Meriden, and gave up my perfectly good life in Kiev, Ukraine.

Oh boy, the light is on in one of my rooms, so I have to go and do what a CNA has to do with her residents.

After changing depends, I went to take my lunch break. It's for about fifteen minutes to eat the sandwich and drink a can of tomato juice. I start thinking back in my life and figuring out where I went wrong and what I could have done to avoid that . . .

My thoughts were too raggedly dispersed that I only ate a half of the sandwich. Another light on other room went on, for another person needed help. Damn!

In my normal and past life, I was an EHS (environmental, health, and safety) engineer and worked for many manufacturing companies as an EHS coordinator, manager, and engineer. Circumstances of my life now placed me with physical work in an old place home as a nurse assistant. It sucks to give up what you love, but you are the one who has to choose your priorities!

How I ended up been a CNA versus an engineer . . . read and find out, because it has lot of truth.

On one occasion in a while, I would lash out, but it's totally the truth and nothing but the truth.

CHAPTER 1

This morning on the One American News channel, I heard that Putin making a speech about the new strategic Russian nuclear weapons.

He said, "The weapons include a nuclear-powered cruise missile, a nuclear-powered underwater drone, and a new hypersonic missile that has no equivalent elsewhere in the world."

I thought to myself, *Gee, he was just working on his reelection two weeks ago for the 2018 election*. Hell, I've heard so many speeches on Russian TV it's not even funny!

I went to take a shower before going to visit my husband in the hospital, and I hope to go to the Apple Grove after the visit. It's a club here in Vernon. We do it every weekend now. The Apple Grove is very homey place, and everybody knows me and Dave. Obviously, the twenty-eight years' difference between our ages has not happened in everybody's life. Well, it happened in ours!

Dave had a couple more amputations, and it took a toll on him. He did not walk too well anymore, and his feet were swollen. So who do you think is the babysitter?

Me, myself, and I!

I was in the shower when I heard a noise that was out of the normal house noise, like our dog Roti's tags dangling or her feet scratching my hardwood floor or her breathing, hacking, burping or anything else that can come out from the rottweiler.

I knew that Dave was in the hospital because I took him there yesterday. He got admitted, and I was hoping to get him out of there today. There's nothing wrong with hoping!

This time I didn't have my gun in the shower because I didn't receive a dead squirrel warning, like the last time a little over a year ago.

I thought, *If somebody is there, I will knock them out with my bare hands if I have to.*

I opened my bathroom curtains and looked outside, and sure enough Yuri stood at the opening of my walkway. I knew he would find me, even if we moved to a different house, but why bother moving all the furniture, clothes, dog, etc. to the new place when I knew, with his connections win the US, he would find me anywhere?

Yuri was my ex-instructor at the academy in Moscow. I went there because of the Chernobyl catastrophe that happened in 1986. I graduated from high school that year. Scientists know that the best thing to limit your exposure to radiation is to put distance between the radiation source and yourself.

I found a new job, and they would pay for relocation, but with all the hassle to move and pack, we considered to stay where we were now.

I mentally slapped myself for not bringing my gun to the shower. If you have a possible threat, like last time when a dead squirrel showed up in a package in the middle of your normal day, you have to be protected!

I'm a lefty, so I thought, *If I give him one of my left-hand hooks and after that with my right hook, he may not ever realize what happened!* Well, I was not in the position to take chances at that moment, so I just tried to relax.

Yuri didn't know that I'm a lefty because in that time in the USSR, you had to be right-handed. My parents had to take me to a specialist, who was not cheap, to get me "adapted to the world around me." I was about five or six years old at that time. They also had to take me to a speech specialist at the same time because I could not pronounce an "RRRRR" like the Russians do. It' almost a rumbling when we say "RRRRR."
I was so pissed at myself that I just mumbled, "What do you want now?" and went to get my glasses.

"Hi, babe." He was standing in the middle of the hall with a big broad smile. I could swear, the sun was reflecting off his ratty and artificially whitened teeth!
Damn, if I only had a gun! I would shoot him right this second, but my gun was in my bedroom on the nightstand.

I was so pissed off that I slammed the bathroom door in his face.

"I'll wait for you in the kitchen," Yuri said after I closed the door.

"Yeah, okay," I mumbled and got my clothes.

CHAPTER 2

I quickly brushed my hair, dressed up in a T-shirt and shorts, and walked into the kitchen.

It was stupid to ask how he got into my house or how he knew I was alone. The first question I asked was "Where is my dog?"

"Outside. I hope you trained her good enough not to run away and get lost. She is a very nice doggy, she was trying to lick me," Yuri said, and he smiled.

"Is that a new dog?" he added with the smile disappearing from his face.

"Yes," I said. "The last one died."

It's hard to come back from a trip and hear that your dog died. Animals break your heart! You love them like kids, but the life expectancy for a large dog is usually less than twelve years. Lappa was eleven, and she died alone at home. It was hard for me to think about it because she died when I was out of the country and Dave was at work. I guess dogs can die from loneliness too . . .

Damn, if I only had my gun, I would shoot this bastard right now!

I remember the last time when Yuri walked to my home—it was the beginning of the end . . .

I took my time and went downstairs and let the dog in.

She is a half rottweiler, half German shepherd, the same as Lappa was. She looks scary but is the nicest, friendliest dog. Just pet her and she is your best friend! She was not a big protector, as you can see, but at least I had one creature on my side now. She immediately ran upstairs and sat down near the refrigerator.

"What's her name?" Yuri asked, scratching her ear.

"Roti," I answered and took a cookie from the jar.

Roti was immediately by my side. What is it with dogs and cookies? I rarely ever get excited about food. I usually eat because my brain tells me to eat to survive.

I don't like my dog being too close to a person who can break her neck without even a twitch.

"Quite a dog," Yuri said.

"How is your wound? I guess you are healed enough to travel," I said and petted the dog. She was a quite a dog; we adopted her from a shelter after Lappa died. I was hoping she would be bit more protective than Lappa was, but my hopes flew out of the window this morning.

I put the dog in my bedroom and closed the door. Could I get the gun just by walking in my bedroom? Yes, but I was also thinking about the mess I would have to clean up after the shooting. Besides, all the neighbors were all awake by now. It would be hard to explain a shot fired in our quiet neighborhood.

I could hear that the dog was pissed after she scratched on the bedroom door like there was no tomorrow. She was missing the party. Oh well, this party I would gladly miss too!

"What the hell do you want, Yuri?" It seemed like that was the start of all our conversations lately.

Last time he walked into our house, I ended up going back to Russia and had quite an adventure, with shootings, prisons, and a love affair.

"You don't need to go back to Russia this time." He stared at me over his glasses. "I need you to do something for me here, in the US, while you're still working in the same company you are working right now."

Jesus, Mother of God, I thought to myself. *He wants me to be a spy! How the hell he found out where I am working now is beyond me.*

I guess now with everything on the internet, one can snoop around and find out everything, from LinkedIn to Facebook.

"I need information on the composition of the board your company makes for defense purposes." He smiled.

Damn, why didn't I grab the gun? To hell with the mess! I thought and slapped myself mentally on my head. With the rate I was slapping myself on head, I could end up with concussion pretty soon.

In my old country, the USSR, we were all trained to accommodate the needs of the government. About 95 percent of the population, in one way or another, was working for the KGB. We even had KGB joke: "The guy calls the KGB and tells the operator that his neighbor eats black caviar. The next day his neighbor disappears, and the guy ends up with extra living space."

"Like hell I will!" I would refuse to do anything for that asshole in the first place, but betraying my country? That would not happen, ever!

He continued, like I didn't even open my mouth, "The board is used to set up an explosion in the air before the bomb hits the ground. It's a defensive mechanism so that if someone decided to bomb the US, it will protect people and structures."

I poured myself a cup of coffee. I was furious! I didn't offer coffee to Yuri; I had enough of him in the past year.

"Remember, I found you!" He winked.

"How do you know I will work with you? Why would I do that? I never even liked you back at the academy!" My blood pressure was going through the roof at that point!

He took a folder from the backpack.

"Remember, I have a lot of information here that could be sent to the INS if you do something stupid." Then he opened the folder.

"I would like you to be more cooperative, or I'll send this to your government," he said, waving the folder. "You became a US citizen only because you lied on your application." He took the copy of my citizen application from the folder and waved it in front of my face.

"Yuri, I had enough of you for the past year. I know what you can or cannot to do now." I was smiling for the first time.

Last year, he came to my house and arranged for me to go back to Russia on a spy mission, where I almost got killed and saw a couple people killed.

He said, "I did some research online, and it said that if you become an American citizen, there will be no more hassles for you. You can be free and safe."

"What now?" I asked.

He was pissed off, I could see.

"Yuri, I'm not working for you on a spy mission, period!" I was getting a little hot by now.

"What about your husband? Does he know?" He started to smile.

"You are a stupid son of a bitch! I told him after the last trip to Russia!" I was actually bluffing, but . . .

I didn't tell Dave what was going on at that time, and I was not explaining my last trip, because as they say, "Easier to ask for forgiveness than permission."

"Get out of here." He was getting on my nerves. "I did some research, and you are not going to ruin my life again!"

He smiled, which was surprising.

"How about your new employer? Do they know your background?" Now his eyes became as hard as a rock.

I swallowed, thinking, *This damn bastard would do anything to get money*. He was my superior at my academy years ago, back in Moscow. Greed was the main motivation for him then, and I didn't see any changes in his behavior now.

"How do you think I will do that?" I was terrified of losing this job, which took me about eight months to find.

"You will manage. I have always known that," he said, and he walked out of the front door.

CHAPTER 3

I thought of following Yuri, but when I looked from the front porch, there was no car or anything to follow. It was like he disappeared into thin air.

I sit for a while, smoking my electronic cigarette. My dog was near me, putting her *morda* on my legs.

I gave up smoking real cigarettes about eight years ago. Now, I gave up cigars after my previous trip to Russia. Giving up smoking was the hardest thing I had ever done. I gave up many, many drugs in my previous life, but it was never that hard!

There was a 7-Eleven right around the corner. I could walk to it, if I came up with a good excuse. Believe me, I always win when I'm arguing with myself!

Oh shoot, I have to stop at the grocery store before I go to the hospital! I remembered it while walking downstairs to the garage. Dave couldn't lift anything anymore. At least I could go shopping, which was our normal routine weekend activity.

I started wondering how I was going find the information that Yuri wanted. I finally made a decision. It was iffy, but I hoped it would work. While starting the car, I made a plan. No reason to tell it to anybody, but I was still wondering if it would work.
Damn, Yuri, I should have killed him on my last trip to Russia, I thought to myself. *I'm not going to get any help from anywhere! I'm on my own.*

In America, it's funny how the law works or doesn't work. If you came here legally to pursue your happiness, you have or have someone else pay money to make you legal. My husband had to pay for my paperwork and sign the affidavit of support until I became an American citizen. I started working almost immediately because at home, all you know is work and work. How on Earth all those illegal immigrants could have food stamps and money to pay for rent is beyond me!

I bought the groceries and put them in the refrigerator. After that, I went to my bedroom and took my gun out. I was thinking of going to the local hotels and finding Yuri. Well, "go fish," as they say in one of those card games, which I never played. I got off that high horse and went vacuuming the floors.

I usually run every tough decision by Dave; he helped me a lot over the years of my career. I did not think that telling him that I had to steal the secret of how to make the defense of my country more vulnerable would be wise. Dave worked for Pratt and Whitney for forty-eight years, more than I was alive! He knew every trick to get the vendors foot in; he was absolutely amazing at every project to got thrown at him! Well, that was why I married the guy!

Our visit was good, and the doctor was releasing him tomorrow. Well, his doctor said, everyone does very well after an amputation on his watch!

The next day we had an ordinary Sunday, and I couldn't sleep that night because my head was spinning of the possibilities and probabilities of me being caught. Taking melatonin had helped.

CHAPTER 4

On Monday morning at work, I chitchatted with couple of coworkers and did some small research on the Russian presidential election candidates.

Holy shit. There were numerous names, but I bet nobody would stand up to Putin in the election in March. I would not vote for my ex-husband (even if I had a choice). He is the one that told me last year that Yuri retired. Now I just saw him, and he didn't look retired to me!

Well, baby, get to work! I told myself. I went downstairs, where we kept the blueprints, and dug out the blueprint of the board. Jesus, Mary, and God—if I can read it. It was not in Cyrillic or in English!

I'm an engineer; I thought I could read anything, but apparently not!

Because at work, we can't have cell phones, cameras, or anything else, except the badge around your neck, I had no means to take a picture, and of course, I didn't think bringing my little camera this morning. Now I have to sneak that print out. But how do I do that?

We have very heavy security, and sneaking out is prohibited! Okay, I thought to myself, what if I make a copy of the print?

Let's find the copy machine!

Aha, good luck! There were no copy machines on that floor!

There was a reason why there was only one clerk and many prints; you don't want anybody, like me right now, copying anything without management knowledge.

Now I have to find Mr. Bricks, who was the housekeeper of that floor.

Okay, I found him on the first floor because he needed to use the bathroom. I had to use the bathroom myself as well; I almost peed in my pants!

Mr. Bricks is a very interesting man. He is an ex-convict; he spent thirty years in prison for murdering his wife. How do I know that? Keep guessing! It's all in his job application, which I "borrowed" at the front desk. I'm sneaky, like that!

I can skulk around for weeks, as they say in English. I meant British English, not American. They are two different languages. Americans abbreviate so much that you can hear only EPA, OSHA, DEP, DOL, and if you don't understand what all that is, you're lost!

CHAPTER 5

It's hard to be a caregiver! Dave can't walk a mile with or without help. And that help was me for the past year. It's been a trip and a half with all his surgeries, his medications, etc.

We were married twenty-five years ago and still took care of each other.

I guess when both of us said "I do," it translated to what I do now!

I was a twenty-three years old; he was fifty one. It was fun when we both could travel and see the world, but lately, it's been hospital after hospital, amputation after amputation. I was hoping that somebody would slap my forehead and ask me, "Why are you doing it?" But at that time, nobody around to do that, so we just simply got married.

I really didn't realize at that time what I was signing away my life for. It was like a dream, but now came the reality check. Oh well, don't we all have to learn from our mistakes? I was working as an engineer for nineteen years; it's time for me to become a doctor!

It's funny, but on the last visit to our doctor, I told him that I would be like him. He became an engineer first, but then he changed his mind and became a doctor. After years of studying, he had his practice, then changed his mind again and decided to go back to engineering. According to him, at that time, it was too late, as he already had a wife and three kids, so he was working awful hours at his practice. I really like him; he knew what he was talking about!

After I do what Yuri wants me to do, I will quit that job and become a nurse. This is my final decision.

Now I just needed to find a printer or a copy machine, and I would be all set with the blueprint. The materials we use for stripping and coating, I would know from the waste that we shipped out. I was the one who signed and kept a copy of that manifest for five years, according to one of the abbreviations, knowing as DEEP.

I have very strong math and physics knowledge, so calculating how much copper, gold, silver, and other chemicals was not a big problem for me.

So, with the blueprint behind my back, I skulked to the main office. I just needed time, when nobody was inside the print room.

We have one common print room, and it was for everybody to share, so people who could come in and see that large print would ask some questions. I'd rather avoid it. Taking that big blueprint would unavoidably lead to questions. So I just waited and watched the room, doing the calculations on my computer. In between, I was doing some other work-related calculations.

CHAPTER 6

Finally there was nobody in the print room, so I ran in and made a copy of the blueprint for Yuri. Okay, one task done!

I went back to the archive, and after a little chat with Mr. Bricks, I returned the original to where it belonged. He had bad eyesight, so sneaking in was not hard for me.

By now I was crashing with a nervous breakdown. I was shivering and sweating, I guess, and it was taking a toll. When you are spying on your company product and your company has a lot of security and a lot of repercussions and if they catch you doing it, it won't be a walk in the park, believe me!

I came back to my desk and started thinking what I was going to do next. If I believed in God, I would pray, but in the USSR, we did not have religion. So, you only have the fear of the government.

It's funny how it is for people; you are either afraid of God or the police, another authority that could penalize you for bad things you have done. In my country, in my days of growing up, there was never a god in presence, but cops were everywhere. I guess it came with the Stalin regime and the Communist party cultural beginnings.

I decided that after that job, I was going to become a CNA (certified nurse assistant), because somebody had to keep Dave in the okay stage, but also keeping my sanity . . . I'm really ugly when somebody is holding me back!

I did my job for the day—reports, scorecards, etc. I went and saw Dave in the hospital. Oh, boy! He didn't look that good. I feared that he might lose his second leg. As an ex-nurse and ex-medical doctor, I can tell you if you have gangrene. To me, it looked like that.

We chitchatted for a while, and I left to let the dog out. The dog was fine when somebody was home, but when Dave went to the hospital and I went back to work, she got a little bit crazy with chewing on everything, like pillows, blankets, books, and toys.

I ate some omelets, watched TV, and went to bed.

I could not sleep, with my brain going and going and going. I was thinking why people kill people, why so many wars are going on, why countries that once were together now hate each other's guts. Ukrainians hate Russians, England is a total mess, Israelis and Palestinians have been killing each other for centuries.

I remember about two years ago my friend and I went to Australia for vacation. During the outback trip, we had a lot of fun. At the end, about midnight, our guide told us to get out of the van and lie down on a highway. Just to let you know, the highways at the outback are not like our highways here; it's about one vehicle an hour one way and maybe two the other ways.

We did, and she turned the van lights off.

Oh my god! We saw the Milky Way so close to our faces all of us tried to touch it. Billion, gazillions stars! It makes you feel like you are as small as a grain of sand in this world. The stars live for millions of years. Who the hell are we to think that our actions would change the outcome of universe?

After crying a little, I took melatonin; it's an over-the-counter medication. I used to take it when I was traveling to different countries in my past life. As an example, when the difference between US and Sydney is fifteen hours, your stomach does not know if it needs food or sleep or what? Good morning after supper, I would say.

All night, I was dreaming about Milky Way . . .

CHAPTER 7

I wanted to write my story about being an immigrant in America for some time, but now the controversy on immigration laws really got me fired up.

Everything you will read in this book is based on my personal experiences and knowledge. I know that we all come to this "melting pot" in different ways and have different experiences, so if anybody disagrees with me, let them write their own book. These are my beliefs and views, but somehow I think a lot of people in this country will agree with me.

My journey began twenty-five years ago in a beautiful city that never sleeps—Kiev, Ukraine. I met my now husband, fell in love, said yes when he proposed marriage (after the third time), applied for a fiancée visa in the American embassy, and started waiting for the interview. We did everything by the book, or at least everything the officials at the embassy told us to do (there was no book in the first place), and we were told that we will receive an invitation for the interview in six weeks. Well, six months later, there was still not a peep from the embassy.

My fiancé had to go back to America for a couple months and wanted to take me with him. But I did not have a visa. At this time I was working as a translator in an American-Ukrainian joint venture, so with a little help from a lot of people on both sides, I received a business visa for six months.

As you could see, I came to this country illegally—or rather, legally to stay and work for six months, but not legally to marry and stay for the rest of my life. Let me tell you about the hoops we had to jump through to avoid deportation and other consequences in the first six months of my new American life!

First of all, we had to get merited in fifteen days after I crossed the American border. Think about that—fifteen days! At that time, I had no credit cards, no friends, no money, no license, and no knowledge of American wedding traditions. Talk about clueless—that was me standing in front of some guy with a funny-looking tie on my wedding day, repeating after him the words I didn't really understand, "For better, for worst, blah, blah, blah." He said to Dave, "Good enough, you may kiss the bride." After that, we had a little party with my husband's friends. That was my big Russian wedding in a New York minute.

After the wedding and endless paperwork, I was waiting for my temporary green card for six months. During this period I could not leave the country because I might not get back. Those were very long six months for us.

What absolutely amazed me later is that I did receive an invitation for the interview in the Warsaw, Poland, American Embassy for a fiancée visa ... three years after I moved here. Two things I want to point out about that. One, good tracking of immigrants we have here! I received a permanent green card that year, but apparently in Warsaw, they still have me on file as a poor little girl who is aging, waiting for her fiancée visa. Second, do they really get that busy there in the embassy that it took three years to process my paperwork?

Let me tell you a little secret here. I know that some people got a visa to this country by paying a couple thousand dollars under the table to American Embassy workers. As an American citizen, I'm ashamed and outraged by this fact. Who in my old country can afford to give a two- or three-thousand-dollar bribe? Not a regular worker, who can barely pay monthly bills, but criminals who get their money by racketeering, stealing, and cheating. Do we want people like that in this country? Do we want people that open our boarders to criminals for personal gain? Something to think about ...

Now a caravan is coming through Mexico—thousands of immigrants from all over the word, with all kinds of religion and hundreds of kids. I don't blame Americans for shouting "No!" and complaining about the security of the US. Whoever wants them to go back home is right.

You want to stay with your children, stay with them in your country, period!

CHAPTER 8

I was in a shower that morning and heard the noise again. "*Good grief!*" I thought to myself. "*Is this Yuri again?*"

I opened the shower curtain, but it was only the dog, standing at the door opening, looking like she ate a squirrel or something else. Happy and smiling!

We just installed a dog door downstairs for her so she can come and go as she wants to. I was worried we might end up with raccoons or squirrels on our couch, but talking with some friends, it shouldn't happen, and it was good to have it.

I got out and pushed the button to start the coffee. I'm not good in the morning without my daily coffee intake! I had about two cups and started my car in the garage. I like to have the garage so I don't need to "unscrub" my car in the morning.

The traffic was heavy, like it usually was in Connecticut and Massachusetts. People rush and run over you to get to where they have to be, like five minutes ago. We call people with MA plates mass-holes because of the way they drive. They call us connadicated because of the way we drive. I guess it comes with the territory!

At work, I felt like a squirrel in the wheel—dig it, dim, and dim it, dim. I finally finished my annual reporting to every abbreviation; you could think of EPA, DEEP, and OSHA. The first of March, everybody's reports were due. I don't even think I ate lunch that day!

I was so tired that my knuckles turned white while gripping my steering wheel so tight.

I came home and let the dog out. I closed the dog door when one of us is not home just as a precaution. She should be okay all day, but in the evening, she had to go pee and poop. I did a little house cleaning and went to see Dave. After a short visit, I had a "just shoot me" feeling. He was going to get depressed. Who would not in that place? I got depressed just walking in and out of it.

I went to the local bar where we used to go after my work. It's actually a German club. Years ago, only German males belonged in it, but now, it was for anybody who wanted to join. I sat down with my favorite crew, and we chitchatted about everything. My favorite "dogs" are Pigeey-Wigey, Shamoose, Roger-Dodger, Silver Foxy, Kuhsi-Woohsi, Wacky-Jacky, and Flopsy-Mopsy.

I have no idea why I named those guys like that; it was just what I envisioned at that time. It was weird for me. Once I name a guy something, it will stay in my head for the rest of my life. It's funny that after a while, people would start calling that person the name I gave him.

In my previous life, I was working with six water plant operators, and I had names for each one of them. Now, years after, they still call me and talk to me. When I ask them "How is Barsuk doing?" they knew exactly who I'm talking about. Barsuk means badger in English. That's one of my ex-operators; I named him that because he looked like a badger.

The truth is it's catchy when you come up with Russian words that mean something else or nothing to Americans. I would swear "Son if a *zaychik*!" when I dropped something on my foot. At work you can't swear because you are in a managerial position. Everywhere I worked in the past, all workers would swear "Son of a *zaychik*!" That means "son of a rabbit," but it uses the same syllables as saying, "Son of a bitch!"

Dave and I love our club because of the people in it! You can talk about baseball, football, news, or anything else. It's social, and it's good to get with other people to bitch about work, bosses, coworkers, etc. Everybody has an experience on something, be it a plumber, a construction worker, or a bar administrator. It's a good mix of people, which works for everybody. Just remember, "experience is what you get when you expect something else," according to Dave.

I also talk to the bartending girl, Cheryl. I talk about my problems, fears, hopes, and everything in between. That's the bartender's job, to listen and agree with you.

Do you know this old joke: What is the difference between the proctologist and the bartender? The proctologist has to look at one asshole at the time. The bartender has to look at all of them at the same time.

After a little complaining and talking to those guys, I went back home.

CHAPTER 9

The next morning I went to work and counted the drums of waste to be shipped today. I also wrote each drum's contents and concentration. That's what I do for a living and everybody at work knows that.

I came to my desk and started calculating. Calculations and converting from gallons to metric liters is not a problem for me. I started converting when I came to this country—I was forced to do that.

In the driving manual that I had to study, before taking the driving test, there was a question: "How far from the curb can you park?" Well, I looked at the answers, and it said, "A foot". I start thinking, "How would a police officer know how big your feet are? Can the people with bigger feet park further from the curb?"

Later that day, Dave came from work, and I asked him that question. He laughed and said, "It's an American measurement. In almost all of Europe, we use meters and kilograms, but over here, most people think in feet and inches." It didn't take me too long to start converting in American versus metric.

It was funny. One day, two of my colleagues were in one of our facilities in Germany. After the trip, one of them was telling us the story about their trip. They got to the store, and one of them told the other one to get the bread and he will get ham and cheese. So, Bobby went and got the bread, and they met back at the car. After the next line, I laughed my ass off—Bobby got two small sandwich rolls, and when he saw how much ham and cheese the other one got, he almost fell on the ground, near the car. That one got a kilogram of ham and a kilogram of cheese! They ate it for the rest of the trip! There were 2.2 pounds of ham and 2.2 pounds of cheese for two people. That's a *lot*!

Anyway, I finished the calculations and was pleased with them. I started thinking about Yuri. I hoped he would be pleased with everything.

Yuri, goddamn! I have to figure out how to kill him! It would be tough to do it in Connecticut or the US at all, but it was possible. I'm sure about that. I went through my kill list, and he won first place. So, I went on with my planning.

How in the hell am I going to kill that bastard? Of course, I could do it, but I didn't want to get up in the morning with police staring in my face. Of course, it was always better than looking at some old and fat bastard in the morning!

Why are most of the police officers fat? There are plenty of jokes about the doughnuts and police! There may be some of the truth in it!

I finished calculating and went home. Enough is enough when you work for the company that pays the salary for your service you provide. Salary . . . Do you know what that means? You work for celery and the carrots!

It's one of the sayings that keep me in my life, take it or leave it: When life gives you a lemon, you make lemonade out of it!

I survived the old Soviet Union show, and I survived to live it in US for over twenty-five years now.

I guess you learn it from the tough place when you grew up.

CHAPTER 10

It's okay to do what I have to do. Whether it's hard or not, whether it's mentally disabling or not, you have to push. It's hard, but you have to push your best because you deserve the best!

If you are writing a book, painting a picture, or doing your job—if it's any one of those, if you believe in yourself, you will do well. Otherwise, forget it.

I had Chinese food takeout the other day, and my fortune cookie said, "People make their own success." I totally believe it.

I push myself every day because I don't want to become a one of those Americans that get fat and floppy with age. Yes, I'm not a spring chicken, but I still have my Russian pride. If there's one thing that Russians will never give up, it's pride!

I told one of my girlfriends that I read what I have so far in my first manuscript today and that I would revive my parents, because in my first book, *Good Morning after Supper*, they were killed in a car crash when I was fourteen. She said, "No way!" I said, "Yes way, there are a lot of funny stories I can tell about them!"

No, they are still alive and well. It took me about two years of paperwork and a lot of money to allow them to come here, to Connecticut. Dave had to call a senator to get it expedited. It's a pain in the ass and ears when you are put on hold by INS!

I enrolled them in a local school and the gym across from their apartment. After almost four years, they still can't say thank you. For the love of God, I don't understand it!

Really, seriously, to say thank you, it's not too hard. I think because it's they grew up in Russia, where it is almost criminal to show how you felt, and for years it was a cultural no-no. They felt too vulnerable to say those words.

Any way, they are here, in a warm and cozy apartment, with membership to the gym and our credit cards. That's all I care about for now.

On the thank-you, I will continue to work on it, believe me! It's a lot of work to change a person when they are almost eighty years old, but if you keep trying, hopefully it will work out. After Dave comes back from the rehab after the amputation of his left foot, I will have my hands full, but it's part of life.

I called rehab an old people's home, as it's too depressing to go in and out and see all those old people sitting in wheelchairs in front of the room drooling and talking to themselves.

Let me tell you, the past two years were a trip and a half for us!

CHAPTER 11

But of course, Putin won the election! There were no candidates running against him. Some of them got mysteriously killed, some of them mysteriously disappeared.

It is life in the old USSR . . . That's why I wanted my parents here in the US in the first place. It's not that they don't have a place to live there, but the situation in Ukraine is different from when we all lived in the Union of Social Soviet Republics.

My parents met in Moscow, when they went to the same academy I went to seventeen years later. Luba (my mom) was in the same profession that I was going at that time, and Dima (my father) went to veterinarian classes.

I started to call them by their first names when I was fourteen. They both did not exist in my life before or after that. That's the reason.

Well, I'll take it back. After the Chernobyl disaster happened, they got me drunk on red wine the first time in my life. I was sixteen. When I turned seventeen, Luba told me to pack my suitcase and go to Moscow.

With radiation all over the Europe, all you can do is put the distance and time between it and you . . . I'm thankful for it!

That's why they were here now. It's not a breeze, but it's a relief for me to make sure they are alive and moving . . . Like I said before, take the lemons and make lemonade out of it!

I went to work this morning and thought, *What else do I need to get Yuri for that board?*

I got the concentrations of the chemicals and the amount, I got the board configuration, but I had a feeling in my gut that I was missing something!

No shit! I didn't write the mixtures of the bases! You don't put a 100 percent of gold in the bath; you have to put some water, some sulfuric acid, some gold. Where can I find this information?

I guess I will have to talk to our production engineer. Not my favorite part of the job, and I have to come with a good excuse to know that information!

After I had my second cup of coffee, I came up with the good excuse. Now I have to talk to the guy! You know what they say, "Suck it up, buttercup!"

That's what I do lately, and it *sucks*!

CHAPTER 12

It's not that I don't like the guy; I do, but talking to him was a challenge! We are all scattered between what is happening in our lives and work. It's like my driving in and out of the garage. That is sometimes challenging for me. Those garage doors can be very sneaky, they can move any time, left or right!

It is the same with this guy. I personally don't like sneaks, but of course, you have to put up with it! I sucked some air in my lungs and went to his office.

He was on the phone, so I signaled okay and left.

I went back to my desk and did some organizational cleaning up. It's not like my desk is not organized; I have folders and files all over the desk, but if somebody asked me where certain paperwork is, I will find it right there! It's just looks unorganized and cluttered, but I know where everything is.

After I filed most of my files, I went to see the same production engineer again. This time I was lucky and he was off the phone. So, I went into his office and plopped onto a chair.

After a little chitchat, I started my ploy.

"My vendor for waste disposal called me this morning, and they have to get the waste configuration on LDR [land disposal recommendations]. Do we have any cooking recipes for our baths?"

"Why?" He was looking at me like I had two heads. "They can do the analysis and determine what's in it," he told me. I told you, he was a slick bastard.

"Okay, I will run it by the vendor and will get back to you if I need more info." I smiled and left his office.

Jesus, Mother of God. Why didn't I think about it! I guess you just get wrapped up around your own problems and don't even think about earlier solutions. But of course, with my problems and the way my life was going, it was hard to think clearly and methodically rationally.

As soon as I got back to my office, I pulled some items from my manifest file for some of the LDRs. It was not on all the waste, but some. It was a good start!

CHAPTER 13

Next, I called our waste rep, Stephanie. She is also a personal friend of mine. We went to CHMM (Certified Hazardous Materials Manager) conference a couple years ago.

"Hi, Steph, it's Alex. I need a couple more LDRs on a couple of wastes."

"Oh, hi, Alex. Can you let me know which wastes you need the LDRs? I will send them to you."

I gave her the waste ID numbers and waste descriptions, which I put together after a lot off digging. "I would also need the prices on how much it cost us for you to do those LDRs."

"No problem, I will send it to you in an email."

I thanked her and hung up.

LDRs are chemical breakdowns of your waste. Based on your vendor knowing how to properly dispose it, it's either recycled or reused or buried it in a landfill. As the manufacturer you are responsible "from cradle to grave" for your waste. The EPA in 1970 came in up with this idea because there were a lot of landfills that need to be cleaned up, but how to pay for it was a big question. So if they find one drum with your company sticker on it, your company will have to clean up the whole landfill. It's called Superfund in the EPA regulations.

One more problem will be solved!

It's stressful, but to get something off your list is rewarding. So I crossed that one off and looked at the rest of my list … depressing, very depressing! How am I going to do all this in time to go home and let the dog out?

Well, I guess I'll manage, as always.

While doing my work and getting my list shorter (which is never going to get shorter, I know from experience), I was also thinking, When is this bastard Yuri going to waltz into my life again?

"Stop worrying, it will not get you anywhere! Your nerves are shot already," I told myself. I knew I will be prepared for the next time!

I finally left my work and went home to let the dog out. After puttering around, I went to see Dave in the "old people's home."

He was depressed and didn't want to eat the food they served for dinner.

"Try this, try that, can you eat it? Blah, blah, blah."

Finally, I lost it! I yelled at him so loud that every nurse on his floor came into his room asking, "Are you okay?"

At this time, I was crying and getting my mascara all over my face. I said, "It's just a little family dispute," and took the Kleenex out of the box to wipe my face. At least, I stopped sobbing by that time.

Dave told me, after all the nurses left, that he got the message! A little victory in my court—not too bad for the end of the day!

I went home, and on that on my way, I bought a cup of soup at the local pizzeria. I had to eat something at the end of the day, and I did not feel like cooking!

CHAPTER 14

I published the book, which cost a lot of money, but I guess it was worth it. The name is *Good Morning after Supper*. It's about my life in the USSR and moving to the US. I felt that everybody who lives here needs to know how hard it is for us foreigners to come here, make a career, get a job, get an education, etc.

I cried myself to sleep every night the first year I moved to US. No shit, it was hard—no friends, no family! Dave was working all day, and I was left alone. I passed that bridge, so I'm okay now.

When we moved to this little town, because I got a job offer on the north side of the state, we did not know anybody. Dave, as a veteran, joined the local American legion down the road from our house. After a couple months, we knew everybody by their names and nicknames.

After work, it was a pleasure to go there and have good conversations and a couple of drinks.

When the snow was melting in our backyard, I noticed something there. It looked like a firepit. I went and looked closer. Voilà, it was a firepit! Around it there were flat stones, and it was actually built from the flat stones.

After Dave came home, I asked him if he wanted to sacrifice some virgins. He stumbled, but after I showed him the firepit, he said, "What are we going to do with it?"

Good question, I did not have the answer to that either!

We went to the club and talked to the guys if anybody needed the stones. One of the members said, "Oh, yes," and the problem was solved! Let me tell you, lifting those rocks were not a walk in the park, but we did it.

Now, after a numerous years, we are still at the club, and everyone is still helping everyone solve their problems to the best of all worlds. We have a lot of people there—some are carpenters, some are construction guys, some are engineers, some are cooks, and some are bartenders. We like our club, and all members are like a family to each other. We celebrate Thanksgiving, Christmas, and other holidays together. We also have some sad parties, where we celebrate life when somebody passes away. It's not a sad party, just a different attitude and atmosphere. It's a good way to send someone off.

After a little while, we got the "other dogs" in the club, and now we have about four hundred members. We are like one dysfunctional family. Good for us and good for them!

You have to pay a fee to become a member, but fees, compared to the prices of the drinks, are absolutely worth it.

CHAPTER 15

Steph stopped by my work, and after a little chitchat, she gave me the rest of the LDRs. Thank God I have very good and reliable vendors! It's hard to find a company you can trust with your waste because it's millions of dollars if they did not properly dispose of it.

In one of our CHMM meetings, we had a case study on a company that pick up the waste from one of the manufacturing sites and disposed of it in underground tanks in a gas station. Well, guess what, the company was caught and had to clean it up, and it's not in business anymore, because it costs a lot of money to clean up underground tanks.

Before she left, I started my own calculations just to make sure they (vendors) did not take a shortcut with the analysis. Never believe in other people; that's what I learned from the old USSR.

After she left, I put the information from LDRs on a separate list to give it to Shithead when he comes to the house next time.

Well, I'll better prepared the next time than I was the last time, I'll tell you that!

I was catching up on my list. Good luck with that! When one thing comes off, a couple will add on. I was like the squirrel in the wheel, which is my life lately anyways.

I went to see Dave after I finished my twelve-hour workday, and they told me that I can take him home tomorrow. Yahoo! Tomorrow will be Saturday, so I will be there at seven in the morning and will pick him up before they change their minds.

I hoped he could adjust to our house. I did a lot of modifications for his wheelchair. One of our friends from the club helped me with it. I was hoping I could get Dave in and out of the car and into the chair. You don't know if you don't try.

Let me tell you, driving a wheelchair, even without somebody in it, is not my strong suit. We will see if I can handle Dave in it! I guess I'll figure out why they put the seat belts on it. Probably for bad drivers, like me.

With the new dog, we have hairballs everywhere. I can find a dog on each of our stairs. I will have to vacuum the whole house before Dave comes home. Vacuuming is not my favorite sport, but somebody has to do it. Our dog is smart when it comes to food, but getting the vacuum with her little *lapkas* will be impossible. *Lapkas* are paws in Russian. That one, everybody at work also knows.

I do a lot of ergonomic assessments for my employees, and I always tell them to bring the *lapkas* in front of the computer. Not many people knows how far you have to put the screen so you can still read the print so as not buy new glasses to read it. It's one of my many hats I have to wear. Like I said before, you work for "celery and carrots."

Dogs are afraid of vacuum cleaners. She was all over the floor getting out of its way. It was actually funny to see her going from one wall then other! When I was done upstairs, I went downstairs and vacuumed there as well. Her hair does not know where to land. When you walk in the house, you move the hair in all different directions.

After I was done, I poured myself a drink and sat down in front of our indoor fireplace. We installed two of them when we moved into this house. It's nice to sit and listen to the roaring fire and be warm and cozy. The dog was lying at my feet with her *lapkas* crossed.

I don't remember when I went to bed; I was absolutely exhausted!

CHAPTER 16

I woke up at five thirty and let the dog out. Your body is programmed over the years to wake up at a certain time. Even if you know it's a weekend, you're still up and going in your regular work time. Okay, the dog is outside and I can take a shower before I go to pick up Dave.

Before I went to the shower, the dog started barking at something, probably the badger, which lives at the back of our yard. I went downstairs and let her in. Not too many neighbors like to hear that noise at almost six o'clock in the morning.

This time I had my gun with me, just in case. I left the door open, and recently, I bought shower curtains, which you can see through. Like they say in the Russian Army, "Better to be over prepared for the worst case that could come than lose the whole battle because you not prepared at all!"

During my shower, I saw some movement in the hall, and it was not a dog. I grabbed my gun and opened the curtains. Sure enough, Yuri was standing in the door opening.

For crying out loud, he had to come today when I am supposed to pick up Dave in an hour!

"Hi, baby doll." He smiled and winked.

"I'm not your baby doll!" I barked back. "Please close the door behind you." I was not showing the "free naked girl show" again!

Can I kill him, yes, but cleaning our house in an hour was out of the question. So I just got my clothes and got dressed. After I walked into the kitchen, with my gun in the back of my pants, I poured my coffee and looked at this son of a *zaychik*. The dog was near me, by my legs.

"So, did you do what I asked?" No smile from this guy.

"I did, but everything is still at work." Actually, I had to figure out how to sneak it out of my office, past the security guard, and get it secured in my car without getting fired.

"Okay, Alex, I will see you later." And he went out the front door.

This time I was glued to the window as soon as he left. I saw him going to the large black sedan in front of our house. I also saw the car plates on that bad boy.

I went to the computer and started to research the plates. There are a millions sites that can get you all the information you need.

I have no idea how we lived without computers or cell phones before! Really, think about it, how would you get to an address without a GPS? In the old days, you would have a map plastered on your lap looking where you have to go and driving at the same time—that was difficult, if not dangerous!

I found the car plates. It was a rental at the Bradley airport under some other name, not Yuri, but it's a good start! I patted myself on the head and got Dave's pickup kit that I made up the other day. When I get him home, I will research a little bit more.

Now time was on my side . . .

Without the documentation for the board, Yuri will not return to Russia. If he does, somebody there will do him in. I'm sure of it!

CHAPTER 17

I got Dave out of that home so fast I didn't even sign release paperwork. They called me later about it. I had to go back and sign it.

Now we had to try to get him onto the wheelchair, out of the stair lift, and into another wheelchair. Pain in an ass, but as I always say, "If you learned one thing in a day, that day is not lost in your life." We start learning and adjusting as we moved through the house.

I was thinking, it's not that I can't tell Dave that I killed somebody, but he always overreacts about getting in trouble with police. One time, I had a fight with a guy here in the US, and my friends pulled me off the guy and locked me in the truck. I called Dave and told him that I had a fight. He was like, "Oh my god! The police! They're going to find you, you could go to jail, blah, blah." Nothing happened, because can you imagine the guy walking up to police and saying that some blond chick put him on his ass with the first blow? I don't think so!

Dave got exhausted in the first hour of our adjustments and went to take a nap. I started researching on the name I got from the web, because if the car was registered to Sergey Porshnikov, there was a good chance that the hotel room would be registered to that name too.

After about an hour, I gave up searching hotels, because no one will list the names of their tenants. I will have to write the hotel numbers and call them one by one on Monday—like I have nothing else to do!

At four o'clock, I woke Dave up. It's not healthy to sleep when the sun is going down, at least that's what they said in Russia. In my scientific mind, it makes sense; you will not be able to sleep at night.

I took Dave to the club, and everybody there applauded when I wheeled him in. It's a good feeling when you are surrounded by good friends! Dave always told me, "You surround yourself with winners, you will be a winner, but if you surround yourself with losers, guess what you will be."

After a couple of drinks, I took him home. We don't watch TV at home, although we have two. It's just not our cup of tea; we'd rather talk and read books. I was happy that he was back home! I made us some supper, and after a little chitchat, we both went to sleep.

He has his room and I have mine; we set it up years ago. I just didn't want to kick him or slap him while I'm sleeping. Some of my bad memories sometimes make me a little violent. Why take a chance!

On Sunday I took Dave to the club and back. I was realizing by now that I was going to be his chauffer, his nurse, his cook, his everything... Damn, did not expect it when my life was organized before the amputation, but what else could I do?

CHAPTER 18

I also want to write about marrying an older person. For crying out loud, Dave is only two years younger than my parents! His son from the previous marriage is two years older than me. Taking care of Dave is almost impossible—well, I very much exaggerate now. It is possible, but you need to know what you are doing . . . I liked Dave, but Prednisone (the steroid) at eighty-five milligram would make anybody insane, and that's what it has done to him.

In real life, Dave was the most passionate man on this planet, but after the doctor prescribed it for him, I have no idea what happened!

He got upset with little things, like the soup is not hot enough, the phone doesn't work right, or I'm not fast enough coming home from work. He was a good-hearted man when I met him (well enough to marry him), but after medication and other drugs, it was almost impossible to live with the man.

So, listen to me, my young friends, think twice before you say "I do," because you will do, and that one you can take to the bank!

The last time I took him in the hospital, the doctor told me that they will have to amputate his left leg. I saw it coming, but it was still hard to hear. Now, he is in rehab and doing well, but it was a lot of work to set up our house for the person with a wheelchair and one leg. I did what I could, but the only way one can tell what's working or not is when you have been on a wheelchair yourself.

Hopefully, after I take him back to the house, we will adjust everything to his well-being.

CHAPTER 19

On Monday, I went to work as usual. While dressing up in the morning and thinking about that big blueprint copy, I wore the largest pantsuit I could find in my closet and a puffy sweater. The bigger the pants, the more I can fit in!

I went into my office and checked my email. I was trying to do some items on my to-do list, but my head was somewhere else. Between meetings, I called a couple of hotels near the airport and asked to talk to Sergey, but no luck. Okay, keep trying, I told myself. If you try and do not succeed, at least you can say you tried.

I went to the bathroom and tried to fit the blueprint under my sweater and in my pants. I spent about twenty minutes folding and taking the bulges out. In the end, I think I succeeded with that task. There was one thing I was sure about—no sitting in my office with that thing in my pants! I have to go to my boss and find an excuse to leave the job early today.

Stiff as a board, I went to see my boss, who was actually very good friend of mine. I told him that I didn't feel good and would like to go home early. It was not hard to see that I was not too peachy, so he excused me and then I went home. I have all my calculations in the folder. It's not the first time I drove with calculations in my car; I think the guard should know that by now. I passed the guard and told him that I was not feeling well and was going home. If he needed any verification, he can call my boss.

I was in the parking lot, when I saw a familiar car cruising around on the street. Goddamn, Yuri! We were not allowed to have any weapons in our car on the premises, so I had left my gun at home. Any car can be searched randomly, so I did not take chances. Let's see who can race who, asshole! Now I started thinking about driving. The edge of the blueprint was getting in my crevice and was starting to bother me. I had to get it out! I went to the back seat of my car and started to unzip. Boy, it took me another twenty minutes to get the blueprint out; it was a *lot* of work.

I finally got into the driver's seat. Everything else was in the trunk. Even if he shot me, it would take time for him to find it! I started my car and waited till I heard the roar of the highway. Actually the highway was not too far from work, so if I could make it there, I'm good!

I waited for an opening in traffic and pulled onto the street and headed for highway, fast. I was hoping to get there as soon as possible. Who cares, in my situation, what the speed signs say! In my mirror I saw that the Yuri's car had turned around, and by now he was following me. I cursed in every language that I knew, but before he got too close to me, I had reached the highway. Hip-hip, hooray!

CHAPTER 20

It was surprising to see all that heavy traffic in the middle of the day. I tuned the radio on. It was caused by a tractor trailer that had gotten into an accident. All the cars were swerving around trying to get past it. I lost sight of Yuri's car in that mess, but I'm sure he will pop up soon to get his information! By the time I got home, you could say, "Take a fork and stick in me." I was mentally and physically done.

I went upstairs; Dave was on his favorite chair in the living room. He looked at me, puzzled, and asked, "Why are you so early?"

It was time for us to have a talk. I poured myself a drink, and I told him about Yuri and the other trip to Russia and spying on my company. I cried, and my mascara was all over my cheeks.

Before Dave started talking, I made him a shush sign and started looking for bugs. I knew Yuri long enough to know this bastard was not going to sit and wait for me to get out of the bathroom without planting the bug somewhere. I found one in the couch and one in the lamp. I removed both of them.

I told Dave he can talk, though I was not sure if I removed all the bugs. I got my bug detector from the bag that Yuri got me almost a year earlier and scanned for bugs. It didn't show any. It's just showed that my husband had an elevated temperature in his right leg. I didn't tell him that, but I thought to myself, "This one is going to be next."

"I knew that you came from Russian descent." He was very calm. "I saw your reaction when I told you about our submarine that had been at sea and how a Russian ship ran over us. You were pissed."

Yep, you're right, our fishermen were killed without warning by a US sub just driving around, looking for a fish to catch. WTF, what were they doing in our waters during the Cold War?

"Well, baby, after I lived in this country for a couple years and you told me about the accident, I realized that we spied on you and you spied on us. It's been like that for many years," I replied.

"During the Cold War, I understood, but now all the media is talking about Russian spies. It's like a crazy subject! I don't get it!" I was getting pissed off at CNN, NBC, and other news channels.

"It's what media does." Dave was still calm. I could see his brain was working. No wonder, after I told him all my stories. "When are you going to see him again?" Dave was looking like he was calculating something.

I told him the story after my work with shrivels. "I don't know the next time he is going to stop by. Today, he was just lurking in front of my work. Tomorrow, I think he can come in here." I lifted my shoulders.

"I will think of something," Dave told me, and I'm sure he will come up with it. He was tired from all that went on today, so he went to bed.

I puttered around, cleaning the house and, in the kitchen, making coffee for the next morning. I let the dog out again, read a chapter in a book I'm reading, the Harry Potter series. Like I said before, we don't watch TV. Both of us would rather read than watch the stupidity of other people.

I'm genuinely surprised at what other people think is entertaining.

I got the dog back in the house, and both of us, Roti and I, went to my room to sleep. It's actually very therapeutic to have somebody warm and fuzzy near you.

It's not like I missed the sex. Well, I really missed it, but in your head, somebody (you) can just block your senses and not even respond to manual or oral stimulation. You just get into the "shut down stage." I can't explain it, but that's what happened to me.

I read somewhere once that "sex is great, but if you find a person who makes you laugh when you are pissed off, that is priceless." I found Dave, and he does make me laugh.

Anyway, my head was spinning from all the possible scenarios. I had to get up and take melatonin.

CHAPTER 21

I woke up as usual at five thirty, opened the dog door so she could come and go out without Dave going up and down on a lift chair, and started the coffee pot. Dave was still sleeping, so I went to the gym for a short but good workout. I came home and found Dave in the living room, sitting on his favorite chair. The dog was lying in front of him. Quite a scene . . .

I go to the gym because I need to get rid of my mental frustration.

Now we need to learn a new morning routine—take a shower, put bandages on Dave's leg, get out of the house, etc.

"Okay," I told myself, "you can't be at work in an hour, so WTF, I'll skip this day." I usually worked on Saturday because production is 24-7, so to get everybody trained and up to for the day, I had to work six days a week.

It took us about two hours to learn the routine. I didn't know anything about wheelchairs before, I'm learning it now!

I still have all my paperwork in the car. The car was in our garage, but knowing how slick Yuri is, it was not safe. Better to be safe than sorry. I brought everything in the study at home and hid it in the closet. Just to make sure nobody would see the print, I put the vacuum cleaner in front of it.

I just remembered that I have to take my father to the DMV next Tuesday. Crap, how many times do I have to take him? I already took him for the written test five times and four times for the driving test. My car can drive to the DMV by itself, for crying out loud! Dima used to drive in Kiev, but now I think he is getting old, he can't see too well or hear too well anymore.

But of course, his English desire a little bit better connection to his brain. The last time I took him, the instructor asked him to read the sign, and he read "Do not enter" and entered it. I laughed so hard on the drive to his apartment that I almost peed in my pants. I can fix a lot of things, but I can't fix stupid.

I told myself if he doesn't pass this time, I'm not rescheduling him anymore. If he can't pass the test, he is not going to drive in Connecticut. He is not a safe driver, but I will make them take the bus to school, where they supposedly are learning English.

If they learned anything, it was to say "Good morning" when I come there before work. I hate not taking a shower after a good workout or even without one. The shower wakes you up and gets you going.

We had to change the setup in the bathroom for Dave and his one leg. It's not cheap or easy, but it's doable, and we have the right people to come in and modify it. What has to be done has to be done. On the other hand, I would rather pay a person I know than a stranger.

Dave and I watched about fifteen minutes of news on TV. It's a joke what they called the news nowadays. Actually, I don't remember the last time I saw the news. It's all propaganda and brainwashing by whomever is in the government right now. The other day, Dave told me that Soviet strategy couldn't work here in the US, and he told me that socialism will not work for us in the US.

Jesus, Mother of God, really? It worked just fine when I grew up!

We had free transportation, free medical benefits, free education from first to eighth grade, free housing (it came with the danger of losing it if something went wrong)—we had it all. But of course, that was if you were a good citizen. If you were not a good citizen, according to the USSR government, your family would disappear overnight.

I remembered when I was maybe three or four, I heard commotion on our fifth floor where we lived, so I walked out of our apartment to the neighbor next door. I saw a man lying on a floor mattress with both of his wrists slashed. I was shooed out by somebody back to my apartment.

Later that night, his family disappeared, including the little girl my age. I never saw them again, and we got new neighbors that moved in the next day.

In Connecticut, we had to pay more than five thousand dollars a year in taxes on our house—for what? To get our garbage and recycles picked up every week!

Now, we had to figure out how to get Dave from the wheelchair into the car. Thank God I'm in good shape! Working out in the gym pays off.

I drove him to the club.

CHAPTER 22

Everybody was very happy to see Dave, even on a wheelchair. The wheelchair made a metal-on-metal noise when we drove; I shivered at every turn and at every bump. It was also very awkward and heavy to put in and out of the car, but otherwise, he could not enjoy his drinks and conversations. That was what he missed the most, talking to different people about different topics.

Dave is an all-around man; he can give you good advice on financial matters, work behavior, or just therapeutic ones. As long as he's good "upstairs," I can take care of him. When the lights go out in his head, I have no idea what I'm going to do.

Anyway, we get our three drinks, and I drove him home. He was going to eat his lunch and go for a nap while I write my second book. You can't be lazy; you have to stay active, like I said before.

That evening, it was getting dark, and the rain was coming. I saw car lights going up and down our cul-de-sac. It's very rare that we see the movements on our street, especially not during the holiday season. Like I mentioned before, there are only seven houses on our street.

I was peeking from inside the house, trying not to be seen from outside. The dog was watching between the drapes, and I was peeking under the dog's belly. Let me tell you, not the most comfortable position you would choose!

It was Yuri's car passing our house! I got pissed off. Should or should I not call the police? That was the big question. At that time, I decided to wake up Dave and ask him that.

When I woke him up, he was not very happy, a bit groggy, and disoriented. "Sorry, baby," I said, "I had to wake you up in the middle of your nap, but I have a question to ask." I explained everything, and I could see his wheels turning.

He opened his dry mouth and asked, "And what would you tell the cops?"

Before answering I got him a bottle of Gatorade. "I don't know . . ." was my real blonde answer.

Do you really know why blondes put shoulder pads on their jackets? "I don't know"—with a little shake of their head, shoulder to shoulder. A little blonde joke!

Dave continued after a couple gulps of Gatorade, "He probably has diplomatic immunity so the cops would not be able to arrest him anyway. In the end, you are going to spill your guts, and they probably are going to arrest you, not him."

I thought about it for a minute or so and totally agreed with him. No cops are needed right now in our house! Cops are good when you need them and could be a bad nightmare when you don't.

I told that to Dave and closed the door from outside his room. I let him nap a little more before I woke him up at four. I went to the window and peeked outside to see where they were.

Yuri's car was still in the neighborhood. Well, we were not planning to go out, so we were pretty safe in the house.

After I woke Dave up at his regular time, I fed him jambalaya that one of our good friends made us, and we watched *Madagascar* on DVD. It was a good day after all!

CHAPTER 23

I'm not working on Sundays, period! So we had a lazy morning with coffee, and I took care of the bandages on Dave's right foot. To me, it was not looking good, and I told him that. I could see he was upset, but you have to tell the truth to a person you care about.

After I peeked through the window and didn't see any strange cars parked on our street, I finally started breathing more easily. It's a strange feeling when you know that you're being stalked. The uncertainty is the hardest part.

I helped my husband dress up and took him to the club at his regular time. The rehab gave him a wheelchair so we didn't have to put miles on it. We left the other wheelchair at the club yesterday. The regular day crew was there, and we talked and laughed during our visit.

After we got back home, I saw someone had gone through our things—looked like somebody was looking for something in our house. I pretty much know who it was and what they were searching for.

After I checked and everything was still in the closet, I told that to Dave. In a while, Dave came up with an idea to connect the cameras outside our house to our phones. The house will be constantly under observation, and we will know when the shithead tries to do it again. In the meantime, because we knew all our workers personally, he told me to give one of them the paperwork, and they will take it out of the house with their tools.

Brilliant idea!

Tomorrow is Monday, and this chick has to go to work. I got the paperwork out of the closet and gave it to Dave. I told him to give it to anybody working on our house in the bathroom tomorrow. They would take it to the club, and it would be in a safe place for now. He also told me to talk to our across-the-street neighbors and have them put a camera on their house so we could actually see ours from a distance.

I went and talked to our neighbors. They did not have any objections helping us out. It's funny, but even they noticed a car constantly driving up and down our street last night.

Dave also said that it would be good to have camera inside the house to see who is coming and how they were looking through our things. I remembered by then a little camera that Yuri gave me at the beginning of this year before my trip to Russia. I went and got it from my lapel. After a short conversation on the location, we both agreed on the living room.

Both of us went to bed feeling somewhat reassured, as we now had a record of what went on and in our house.

CHAPTER 24

It is Monday morning, and it sucks already. I let the dog out and started the coffee, kissed Dave goodbye, and jumped into the car. Funny how you know that someone was in your car besides you. I don't know, if it's like there was a foreign smell or something...

"Good girl," I told myself and pulled out of the driveway.

It's very interesting, the American language—why do they call it a driveway, not the parkway? You can park on a driveway, right? In New York, they have parkways designed to drive on them.

That was my thought on the way to work; can you imagine my thought on a way from work? Total nightmare! I'm an engineer, but of course, everybody has their own problems.

I printed out my resume at work. Why would I use my own paper? Soon I need to apply for the nursing assistant course. This f——— bullshit with industrial espionage had me absolutely out of shape, mentally, I mean.

I searched online at home for a place to take the course. It's not like I needed another job or another career, but I can try anything once.

I found the course in West Hartford, and it was not too long or too expensive. I called and left a message that I wanted to take this course and wanted to be a CNA.

I didn't even know what was involved in it, but I took a lot of biology and chemistry courses in my earlier life, so I was pretty comfortable taking it and passing it.

Dave was in a lot of pain, so I gave him the pain pill. He actually asked for the phantom pills for the phantom pain, but I gave him a real pain pill and got him to his chair. Five minutes later, he was asleep with his mouth wide open. I was hoping he would stay like that all night.

It's really tough on him not to be able to sleep during night. I could see the big bags under his eyes and the bluish color of his skin.

That night, I saw the car lights between our drapes again going up and down our road. I was more frustrated than ever. "What the hell is he is doing at the open end of our street?" I went and looked out the other window and saw him going from our street to the cemetery, turn around, and come back up our street.

F—— him! He can spend his fuel and add miles to the rental car if he can't sleep! I went to bed, angry, but if you can't do anything, why bother going on circles in your head and deprive yourself of a restful sleep?

CHAPTER 25

The next morning, I got up as usual, fed the dog, and went to work. Oh well, when that's your daily routine, you do it like a robot.

I finished my second book at work, please don't tell anybody! Somehow I have to ... There is a lot of truth, but there was a little fiction there. You decide what and what is not.

I also printed it out at work. Why bother at home, I was busy enough when I came home at night.

I'm not a professional writer. When I have the idea in my head, I have to write it right then; otherwise, it will get sidetracked to another work project.

After I came home and taped Dave's right leg, I took him to the club. At least he will have his social visit for the day.

The leg did not look good, especially his big toe. It looked like it had gangrene to me. I was thinking about it during our social time out, basically all evening. You can't fight gangrene; you can't postpone it or reverse it. We were looking on another amputation. That was my verdict, and unfortunately, I knew what gangrene looks like and smells like.

During our training, in the academy, we had to learn a lot of symptoms and cures for a lot of illnesses, but gangrene was not one of them. There was simply none but amputation.

After we came home, I made Spam and eggs for him and me. We both were in the military, and both of us like Spam.

I know, I know, a lot of people have probably tried Spam once in their life and swore never to eat it again, but I remembered when you eat oatmeal every day for breakfast, lunch, and dinner, a little meat now and then is not too bad. These memories will haunt me for the rest of my life!

Dave went to sleep, and I was watching outside and reviewing what was on the recordings on our cameras. I saw that son of a *zaychik*'s car passing our neighborhood, but because Dave was home, no intruders came in.

"Good Lord, when is this shit going to end!" I had to get up early tomorrow, so I went to bed.

I didn't sleep too well all night, tossing and turning, with the different scenarios running again. I woke up in the morning feeling tired and completely fogged, like I had way too much to drink yesterday, which was not true.

I did my early daily routine, and on the way to work, I saw a different car following me.

Hunt, I thought. *More players and hunters on my ass or perhaps this asshole Yuri just got a new rental.* I will research that pretty soon or recognize the car, at least, when I see it again.

At the parking lot, I looked at all my mirrors, and the camera was recording. Nowadays they have safety cameras you can install on your windshield. It records where your trip went, and in case you had an accident, the cops can see the whole story on it. Pretty cool!

It's funny, but in US, anyone can be prosecuted for a slight crime, except the illegal immigrants that you hear daily on the news. The churches are full of them all over the country. On the news you can hear them protesting the deportation of one guy or another because they don't want to be separated from the other family members. Well, I have good news for you; this a good paragraph, but it doesn't belong here.

Send them all home to Honduras or Mexico or whatever country they originally came from. You still will be together, just not living on the US welfare system, so pay your own bills! The One America News actually counts how much it costs taxpayers for the illegal immigrants. The amount is astronomical, in tens of billions of dollars!

It just irks me how the illegal immigrants come to this country and how they get food stamps for free groceries.

In recent cases, how stupid could one be to look over child porn! Driving around the cities and depositing your wife's belongings and think that no cameras can take a shot of your car?

Are you people so on drugs or hashish or both that you can't even think that you are constantly on camera?

CHAPTER 26

Dave talked to our contractors, and they agreed to take the sketch and my calibrations out of our house. That's the good news! Like people always say, "Out of sight, out of mind."

In my case, I was still thinking about that bastard, no matter what I was doing. It's like having Damocles's sword hanging out of the hair on top of one's head. It will be hanging until I get a solution to get rid of it, permanently. But of course, how? That's the number one question . . .

Okay, I had a revelation about a solution just now. How about I mess with his car and he can have an accident on the road? Not a bad solution, I thought. I just have to figure out how to get to his car and not been seen by anybody or get the right car versus messing up that car with somebody else's. Brilliant, I thought, just brilliant!

Now I have to come up with the plan and work on it. Don't get me wrong, I'm not a delicate flower. I learned my tricks at a young age, but

I had to figure out what can protect me from the open gun fire and come up with a different identity.

I'm blond, and blondes don't look too hot in orange. I really didn't even want to research what color the uniforms the inmates were wearing these days in prison. The same goes for stripes, not my look at all.

I finished what I was doing and drove home, constantly checking my mirrors. *It f—— sucks to be a prey, not the hunter,* I thought to myself.

I didn't see any suspicious activities behind me, so I assumed Yuri was somewhere else, threatening some other girl for something else he needed.

When I got to our house and drove into the garage, I don't know what happened, but those sneaky garage doors got a lot sneakier. So, I hit it! After I finally parked in the garage and looked at the damage I had done to my car, I went inside the house, motherfucking all way to the main floor.

Dave told me that the whole house shook. I told him about the damages and the level of stress.

"By the way, how much did he tell you he will pay you for this secret?" Dave asked.

Holy crap, it had not even occurred to me to ask Yuri! I was standing in the middle of the room speechless.

"Well, include the repair bill in your asking price," Dave told me and smiled.

Jesus, Mother of God—who would come up with this line? If you asked me, my husband was the answer!

God, I love this guy, I thought to myself.

And most of us don't believe in God anyway. So I just picked the right husband for me, yahoo!

I'm taking care of the guy in the nursing home today. I have no idea how old he is, but he told me that he's been married for sixty-three years, and she calls him to tell him good night every night. It's not that a big of a question. Why don't young kids understand or have a value for expressing love and think of the future or build a dream in front of your life to be?

CHAPTER 27

I took time to research the guy who was on the rental agreement for Yuri's car. I also researched the second car's license number. Funny, his name was Michael Gorbachev, like that motherfucker of one of our ex-presidents.

That one I didn't have a problem with, but with everything Yuri has, I don't think he would get the ex-president to chauffer him around. On the other hand, maybe Yuri has a wild imagination and came up with this name for him?

It's funny now that I was looking back at our life and remembering what we went through. Jesus, Mother of Christ, it was the time!

When the USSR folded, every republic went separately and had to elect their own government, their own members... What a mess it was!

Our Ukrainian currency was shooting up every day in hundreds of coupons—the Ukrainian currency at that time.

To pay for our new kitchen furniture, I had to have five million coupons in my purse. I did have a gun on me, but I still was scared with this much money in my shoulder bag.

Now I started searching my soul. Why was I so tired all the time? I came to the conclusion, and remembered not going through a psychologist, on my own: I'm just tired of being tired. That's all, case closed!

Everybody depends on me: Dave depends on me, the dog also depends on me, my parents depend on me, the job depends on me, and now Yuri puts extra pressure on me. It is a lot of dependence and a lot of pressure. I have no clue how I survived this long! There's been almost two months to get back in the saddle again.

I told myself, "One problem at the time." I can only deal with one problem; otherwise, I was going to break, and it's not good for my health or my mental situation.

One of my girlfriends, Sarah Ritter, on our last CHMM CT Chapter meeting told me that she published a book recently. I ordered it online, and one of her poems caught my eye. It is called "Choices."

> Now I say to you, my precious girl
>
> Whose eyes are wide with tears
>
> "Be who you are and be proud of it
>
> Don't submit to your own fears."
>
> Remember you don't need anyone's approval

BUT OF COURSE

Your choices are your own

Years from now, you'll reflect upon your decisions

And realize *My, how I have grown!*

I realized that my decision to mess with Yuri's car was not as good as I first thought about. What if he gets in a wreck and hurts somebody or even kills them!

I couldn't live the rest of my life with the guilt of doing it. Besides, I have no idea what car he is riding now, and in a car wreck, the driver usually dies too.

Not that I felt sorry for the driver because he may have kids and a wife, but if you choose to play that game, you should be prepared to die.

Anyway, I need to rethink my "brilliant" plan.

CHAPTER 28

I saw the lights of a car driving on our street again, and a new revelation came to me right then.

What if I put the silencer on my gun, shoot out the tires on that car, and take Yuri out of the car under the gun! The street is very rarely traveled, and if our neighbors see something, I don't think they will be alert, especially if I do it late at night, in the dark.

I think I like that idea better, but I still will have to run by Dave.

Dave and I went to take a gun safety course and got our gun licenses a couple years ago, when it said on the news that you can't even buy ammunition without a license. That pissed off a lot of people in Connecticut, including us. So we took an official training course and had to wait for three months to get fingerprinted for the licenses.

At that time, we were not even sure if we got to fit into the schedule for the day, which had a lot of people waiting in the police station. One police officer actually told us that he never saw that many people at his station at one time for fingerprinting.

I have a gun permit, and if someone called the police, I would say that I was shooting a woodpecker!

I was sure they would also have silencers on their guns, but at the practice range, where we shot a couple rounds last week, you couldn't hear in it in our house, but you definitely could hear the pops. Our house was located not too far from the range, so during a regular practice we can hear the gunshots—not too loud, but it's pretty obvious.

I just needed to talk to our neighbors and not to scare the bejesus out of them.

It's a stretch, but it might work. It will let me get a chance, for once in my life, not to be afraid anymore!

I went and talked to our neighbors Hans and Lotte at the house on the cul-de-sac. We have known them since we moved here. They are in their eighties, both from Europe, and they understand what you have to do to become somebody in the new country with a new language, new culture, and new traditions.

I walked to their house and told them of possible loud noises during some night this week or next week. I didn't tell them that I would try to shoot someone's tires out, but I told them not to call the police. I just told them that I will be shooting at the tires, not the person.

After talking a little more about the paintings Hans finished lately and the ones I was working on, I walked back home and started thinking about what I will do with Yuri in my custody or with his car and the driver on our street.

Hmm, I can't shoot both of them with my gun because it's registered to our household. I could call AAA and get the car towed to the nearest parking lot as long as there was no blood in the car, because the cops would be knocking on every door in our neighborhood.

There are only seven houses on our street, so I couldn't even think that our house would be missed. Even if I put both of men in the closet, you can't swear the police will not look around. Well, I have time to prepare and make good decisions about it.

What if it's not only Yuri and the driver in the car? I will have to set up a meeting with him and make sure whether he does have or does not have bodyguards.

Yuri is not leaving the country until he gets what he was sent to for, and I was tired of not sleeping every night.

I called Ramsan, my friend from when I was a student, and asked him to get an unmarked, untraceable gun as soon as possible, and I will call him before my departure to Russia.

But of course, he was shocked to hear my voice.

"Babe, I have your old one, remember?" he told me after the shock wore off.

"Oh shoot, sorry, Ramsan. With all the things going on, I don't remember if I even ate last night!"

I don't remember the last trip to Russia so well because it's just easier to erase it than analyze it. There were some shooting, some bloody details, some fighting, and now I remembered that I dropped my gun at Ramsan's apartment before returning to the US. Sometimes I can still taste Dmitri's blood on my lips . . .

We didn't talk any further because one never knows if somebody else is listening to your conversation.

It's just much easier to kill on Mother Russia's soil than here.

CHAPTER 29

Later that day, I went to the club and retrieved my calculations and the copy of my blueprint.

I casually asked a couple of my "dogs" if they know somebody who knows how to fly an airplane. After a few brutal jokes on the matter that "Alex is looking for new husband," Shamoose said that he flew a private plane in Colorado to rescue stranded mountain climbers.

We talked in low voices for a while so nobody else would hear us. Before I left the club, I knew what I had to do next.

I came home and put the blueprint on our study table. I examined it totally, and I could see why it was so complicated for me to make any sense out of it at work. I was just in nervous shock, plus I was under a lot of pressure!

Now, I could see the dimensions and the parts that were mentioned here. When Dave wakes up from his nap, I can ask him how I can alter it without raising any suspicions from my "dear Yuri."

After Dave woke up, I asked him how to alter the print without anybody easily noticing. Dave, after a little thinking, told me to put white paper on numbers and put it on a microchip.

Holy crap, why didn't I do that in the first place rather than lugging it out of work in my pants! Never mind, they already have all the blonde jokes!

I took a picture of the real copy of the blueprint, then I typed in random numbers on the piece of paper and put it on the blueprint. I took a picture of it for my defense (if I ever might need one), but it's good to have evidence. Now, I can destroy the real copy and sleep better at night. After that, I called the number Yuri gave me a year ago for a fake IBM sale representative and told the secretary that I needed to talk to him, so he can call me on my cell. Now I need to figure at what time and where I can meet him.

I was thinking it should be a public place, maybe a bar or restaurant. I came up with one not too far from our home, Wood and Tap.

By the time my phone rang, I had all the plans lined up and was ready to roll! But of course, my head was spinning, and I could barely speak to that son of a *zaychik*.

"Hi, I was not expecting you to call so fast!" I tried to keep my voice from trembling.

"Do you have the info?" I could tell that he was pissed.

"Let's meet at the restaurant near my home this Saturday. I will bring what I have so far." I was sucking on my e-cigarette very hard.

"What time?" he replied.

With everything going in my life right now, I had no idea what would be going on in another hour, so I said, "Give me a call at about nine o'clock Saturday morning, and I will tell you. By the way, bring the money with you, and just to tell you ahead, you owe me two more thousands for repairs on my car." Without even listening for an answer, I hung up.

I had to look for a pilot and crew uniforms and see how much it is for a one-day rental of a private airplane. I also needed to see what the schedules from the airport look like and so on.

By the time I was done in front of the computer, I was exhausted mentally and physically.

That night there was not a lot of traffic on our street, so at least I could sleep without keeping one eye open.

CHAPTER 30

I finally talked Dave into amputating his second leg. He resisted, but it was that or his funeral.

I took him to the hospital and told his doctor to do the same as the first one, except no slicing and dicing this time.

I went to work, and after a usual "squirrel in a wheel" day, just before I went home, I filled out the application for an institute course to become a CNA after the state exam.

Next morning, I took Dima for his final driving exam, and after the normal excruciating waiting time, I was told by the instructor that he flunked again.

On the way home, I told him that he will not drive in Connecticut (or in US, period) without a Connecticut license. He was pissed! But of course, I heard the endless "they did this and he did this," nothing was his fault. This time I was done with him trying to get the state license.

This time, I glanced at the rearview mirror and didn't see any tail after us. Good Lord, finally I can stop being so stressed!

I dropped him off at his apartment and went to work. On my drive to work, I was thinking it's not true that wealth makes people bad. Wealth makes people free and better at treating others.

In the communistic time in USSR, it was not a very good idea to show that you have the money for a car or summer house, jewelry, or fur. They were constantly reminding us from kindergarten that rich people are snobs and mean.

Wealthy people are not that bad, but to get a good-paying job, you need to have an education and work hard to get through the ranks. You have to be able to put your experience on resume, have references and so on, and be able to present yourself.

The poor people are worse off. They are just looking to get food in their stomachs. They have to work hard for very little pay, but they would have to do it to provide bread on the family's table at night. They are the ones who get hot like iron at work on the mission and don't give a damn about other people's needs or trusting anybody. That's how my parents grew up.

It irks me that after all that driving and my very valuable time waiting, Dima still didn't tell me thank you before I left for work. Go figure!

It's funny how it works in this country. Between taxation and social security and immigration laws, Trump wants to end "chain" immigration. I think he should, but again, it's only my opinion. If I did not bring my parents from Kiev to US four years ago, they would probably have gotten robbed and killed by nationalistic fanatics.

If you do everything by the book, you get screwed. I did everything by that book, and they have to wait five years to get food stamps.

One time I asked Dave, How the hell do all those immigrants get their food stamps right away? He told me it was because they gave birth to a kid on our soil; that's why he or she automatically became an American citizen by birth, and they get to have their food stamps immediately.

Well, my parents are too old to give birth to another kid, so I guess I will have to provide them with shelter and food. And that includes their furniture, their kitchen appliances, their bedding—for crying out loud, their "everything plus" program! They still can't say thank you because of the USSR cultural brainwashing.

Finally I got to work, and my "squirrel wheel" started to move.

Because of the nature of my work, I had no idea if I'm going up or down, left or right.

Theodore Roosevelt said, "Believe you can, and you're halfway there."

That's exactly how I feel every day; I'm halfway there.

CHAPTER 31

Finally the work week was over! I had to work half a day on Saturday because I took a half day off to take my father to his unsuccessful driving test. I was at work when my phone rang.

"What time and where?" Yuri's voice was on the other end of the line.

I looked at the number, but it was listed as restricted. Damn!

"At Wood and Tap restaurant, at sixteen hundred," I answered and hung up.

Since Dave wasn't at home, I could put all my rental uniforms there the night before. The rented airplane Cessna was in the airport hangar and was ready to go with a full fuel tank. I hope I covered everything that needed to be covered.

I called my "dogs" and told them the plan goes on tonight. I also told them where we were going to meet. I hope everybody has reliable friends like I do; otherwise, life is not worth of living!

I came to the restaurant early, and because we had a nice day for a change, I was sitting outside, under the umbrella. At this angle, I could see both entrances to the parking lot, which was very helpful in my situation.

I ordered a drink because my nerves were a little shaky. When the waitress came with the drink, I saw Yuri's car roll into the parking lot. After they parked, both back doors opened. Yuri and some other dude walked into to the restaurant.

Okay, so driver is the third one. He was still in the car. Damn, now what do I do?

Early that morning, I packed a vial with the dissolved Percocet, which I took from our safe at home. It was prescribed to Dave after his heart attack last year. I also added morphine and a couple of Valium pills to the mix. I took the bullets for both of my guns and soaked them in that tranquilizer.

I have no idea what the concentration of the potion I "cooked" was, but theoretically, it should be strong enough to knock even a big man out.

Just in case, I put my .38 in my pants and nine-millimeter Beretta in my sock. Right now, I hoped nobody walking behind me will notice the gun in my pants. I wore loose top and jeans.

When I walked into restaurant, I told the cashier that I was expecting company and will be outside. I saw Yuri and his bodyguard looking at me from the door opening.

Let the game begin!

CHAPTER 32

Finally, after the regular greetings and drink orders, we were alone at the table and could talk. At the nearest table, people were eating and drinking. Like a normal Saturday, that place was packed.

I had already texted my guys about the driver parked outside, so hopefully they will take care of him.

"I got this info for you," I said and put the paperwork and a microchip on a table.

Yuri looked through my calculations and told me he will get back to me after looking at microchip.

I wanted to shoot him and his bodyguard right here, but I thought, What if he had diplomatic immunity? Besides there were too many witnesses around.

While we politely kept chitchatting, I put my open vial in my left hand and texted my helpers to come in now.

When the door opened, a couple drunken sailors came onto the patio with a lot of noise, moving unsteadily. Yuri and his bodyguard had to turn over their shoulders to see what the noise was all about. I dumped half the bottle in the bodyguard's drink and half in Yuri's.

Funny, they both had hands on their right hip, so I already knew where their primary guns were.

When they turned around to face me, the bottle was back in my pocket. I smiled and proposed the toast "Na zdorovie!" and lifted my glass.

Yuri was still not at ease with the sailors behind his back, but the American culture is different now than it was described in our books from the academy. The Russian culture is deep in our veins.

So, both of the men replied "Na zdorovie" and drank from their glasses. I had no idea how potent the potion was, so the only way is to stall for time and wait to see their reactions.

CHAPTER 33

The sailors settled down and were drinking beer at their table. Once in a while Kolya, the bodyguard's name I learned in our conversation, would glance back at them. Kolya, short for Nicholas, was a big guy, so I assumed we'd need another drink.

When the waiter came to our table and asked if we wanted a refill, I told her that I would have another one. I offered to pay for their drinks as well.

Knowing Yuri's cheap character, I was almost positive he would order one more for the road.

The sailors were making more noise now, and knowing the Russian culture, I knew that my "friends" at my table were feeling uncomfortable.

After the waiter brought us another round of drinks, I said, "Yuri, you will need to get a special machine to view that microchip. I hope you know where to find it."

"Yes, I know." He was very serious; I would say even concerned.

"I can help you with that, if you want." I was watching his eyes for a sign of fatigue.

When they both turned around again to look at the latest distraction, I put another bottle of the concocted potion into their drinks.

We did another toast, "Na zdorovie." One can't have enough good health; that's why in Russia, it's a common toast.

"Where is the money?" I asked, when suddenly my phone rang. I excused myself and walked out to the lobby before answering it.

It was my parents; they were going back to Kiev tomorrow. Anxiety—you can't believe!

I was just very happy. Now I had more time to see exactly when my potion starts working, unlike with radiation, when time and distance were working for me.

I assured them that I would take them to Boston tomorrow, and they should be all set as long as they are packed and ready to go. I also peeked outside and saw the car Yuri came in when they came to the restaurant. I was just hoping the driver was all taken care of. At least, I didn't see any movement inside the car.

After I came back to our table, I found the sailors talking to my guests at our table. I smiled and sat down.

"How do you do, ma'am?" one of the sailors asked. I bit my tongue so as not to say, "Very well, Shamoose." I just said, "Very well, thank you!"

I could see that my guests were already under influence, so I asked the waitress to bring shots of vodka for everybody.

I almost never drink vodka in America because the vodka you can buy in the store does not taste right. Our vodka does not have an aftertaste and goes down like water. I tried all different brands, and I think they're all still pretty crappy.

Let's take Belvedere, for example. What the hell do French people know about vodka?

Did you know that Smirnoff and Popov are the same vodka? It was in one of my marketing books as a sample of how manufacturers can market the same items for a different population level.

It was cheaper for them to pour Popov in different bottles than build a new equipment line to produce cheaper vodka.

So, I ordered a Ketel One because it's as close to a Russian one as I've ever tried in the US.

After we received our shots, we did another toast and had some of the hors d'oeuvres that I had ordered earlier. I poured my shot to the unofficial tree base near me. I learned that from Luba, my mom, because she used to do this during her working days. When there is a party or meeting and you do not drink, just find a place to pour it and you were all set.

As far as I can see, everybody was getting buzzed, and that was good, but one of us would have to drive. I'm not a very good driver in the first place, but I'm not stupid enough to try to drive drunk.

After another toast, I decided that was a good time to move into action. I paid our bill and walked outside the restaurant with Yuri and Kolya while texting my friend to get into the driver's seat of their car.

The respond was almost immediate: "I'm ready to roll."

CHAPTER 34

After shaking hands and saying goodbyes, they left. My fellow sailors came in, and I told them to take my "Russian friends" to my house.

A week ago, I asked my friend Jojo to get me a tank of the nitrous oxide; she did deliver it to my house yesterday after work. She works at Airgas; the company makes them for numerous distribution centers, manufacturers, and dentists. It's called laughing gas; many of us experience it at dentists'.

I walked outside to the parking lot and was not surprised to see two sailors getting to the back door of Yuri's car. I thought, *Let them experience how I felt in Irkutsk about a year ago, when two strange men got in the taxi I was already in and tried to kill me later.*

Yuri got me sent back to Russia about a year and a half ago. He told me to go into different places and almost killed me, because he was greedy and I didn't know enough about the laws in US. Now I knew a lot more and was prepared to face the problems with solutions. I got into my car and drove home.

I saw Yuri's car on our driveway. I pushed the remote control to open our garage door and let them pull in.

I pulled in another garage door; a two car garage in our house. This morning I parked Dave's car on the cul-de-sac at the end of the street. I closed both garage doors before I even got out of the car.

Never mind of screaming; I don't want neighbors to hear the shooting because I really didn't know if the guys took their pistols out or not.

I got out very carefully of my car and opened the door to the house. I waved my hand for the guys to come in, and both doors opened immediately. The driver door was still closed.

Shamoose showed me the gun in his hands, and Pigeey-Wigeey did the same. Thank God they were not the amateurs in this game! We got this far, but it was a rocky road so far . . . I had to research a lot more, but I did not do it using our computer, because everything you type in your Google browser will be saved as a cookie, and researching what I have to do would get the police involved faster than you ever thought.

I patted down both Yuri and his bodyguard's legs for the second gun and got a small Berretta on Kolya. I placed it on the back of my jeans and told the guys to bring both of them in our study on the second floor. Roti was going wild, having so many guests at once.

The chauffeur door opened, and I saw Rodger-Dodger with the grin out of the car. The last one who came in his truck and parked on our driveway was Flopsy-Mopsy, still wearing his sailor's uniform. I greeted him and went to get gas masks ready for our "old friend."

While talking to Jojo, I learned that the gas will wear out in couple minutes after you take the mask off, but you almost can't overdose on laughing gas.

So we had to work fast and finish the game before I have a nervous breakdown from stress!

"What did you do with the driver?" I asked my crew. Not that I want to know, but good leaders don't leave any possibilities out with the good probability of getting caught.

"He is in the back of the car," Roger told me.

Okay, I have to take care of that, I thought to myself.

I took the gun I took earlier from Kolya, put on the Tyvek suit I brought from work to paint my kitchen (hadn't happened yet), wore gloves and work boots, and with Totolos got in the car with the driver in the trunk.

While adjusting my seat to drive (those of us who ever rented the car knows what I'm talking about), I found a suitcase under the seat. I looked at it and decided that I will open it when I'm back from my dangerous trip.

I drove to the forest not too far from our house, near the shooting range. I stopped, listened, and looked in every direction. Nobody was in scene. I pretty much knew what happened during the disposal of the driver, but when I get back, I would need to confirm it with Roger.

The driver was still out of consciousness; it was not too bad getting him out of the car.

I got him on a bank of the little stream, put his hand on the revolver, and looking in his puzzled eyes, I put the barrel in his mouth and shot simultaneously with guys on the range.

A la guerre comme à *la guerre.* "In war as in war."

I pushed the body with the gun still in his hand, took the suit off, and drove home. Later I will have nightmares about it. WTF, one more to block in my head, like I do many others from my past life, but right now I had to focus on the task at hand.

CHAPTER 35

I bought five pilot's uniforms for for men and one for women. Amazon will deliver in two days; that's why everything we have in our house came from there. Dave bought everything from there. Too bad in his rehabilitation place, he couldn't get a web reception; it's even hard for me reach him when I call him on his cell. He was going out of his mind from doing nothing, but they told me he will be here for another week or so.

So, I put a mask over the bodyguard's face, and before I put one on Yuri, I asked, "Who is behind the plan?"

He hiccupped and said with the smile, "Whoever will pay for it. The bombs keep detonating all over the world, and everybody is eager to protect their children. You know how it works." And he hiccupped again.

I thought about this for a second, and he was right. Russia has very smart engineers and scientists and could develop the similar equipment. The other countries, like Iran, Iraq, Guatemala—God, you can name half of the world here—don't have the leisure to dick around in their free time. It's much easier to pay money to the douchebags like Yuri and get what you need with minimum damage. Knowing Yuri, he doesn't have any morals, except money!

"Do you have a final wish?"

"Go to hell!" He shook his head and hiccupped again.

"Okay." I was done pleasing everybody and their mothers at that time, so I put the mask on his face and saw him drift away.

Before we had to transport those guys, we had a lot of preparation done, so I gathered my helpers around the kitchen table.

"Roger, I assume the driver never walked outside the car in front of the camera, correct?"

"But of course. I gave him an injection and pushed him through the back seat to the trunk. He was heavy, like a big bag of potatoes," he said massaging his shoulder.

"Shamoose, do you have a valid ID for flying? Show it to me, please." He showed me the valid ID in the official badge holder. I was so pleased and started breathing again!

"Can you walk without the limp for five minutes, Flopsy-Mopsy?" When I received an "I will do my best," I told them I needed to go to the library and research something.

"I will be back shortly!" I left with a breeze in the air that the end was near!

After I left, I went to see Dave, and after I told him everything, his suggestion was not to even try to fly to Russia, just exit the plane with the parachutes and let them be discovered by the police in a crashed plane. Okay, now I had to research the insurance on a rented plane.

Well, it's a good idea, but now I would have to check my renting policy because I just rented the plane; I didn't want to buy it!

CHAPTER 36

After a little research, I found out that if I crash the rented plane, I have to pay my deposit and the full price that I already paid up front. It cost us about three thousand dollars per hour plus hangar expenses, plus paying the fuel that was expensive as hell.

Okay, good to hear it! Now after that research, I didn't have to buy a plane—just eat our expenses, which I already figured out are gone. We will have to push them out of the airplane and take the plane back to the hangar. Dave and I don't have three millions to pay for the plane, period.

Now, I had a plan to get them both into the airplane without anybody noticing.

I came back to the house and explained to everybody what we have to do. We had to change from one piece of clothing to another fast. I didn't want our prisoners to get overdosed.

According to the website, one can't overdose on laughing gas if the individuals are healthy. To me, they both look healthy, but with Yuri's recent operations after I shot him, I did not want to take any chances.

There was nothing on TV about suicidal shootings lately, which suggests that the police hadn't found the body of the driver yet and linked it to anybody. Better be broke than spend the night in jail! That's why I have to take Yuri and his bodyguard somewhere else, other than Connecticut, so as not to elevate the suspicions of the police.

I called the hangar and told them that we were coming to take a ride. They said no problem and to just push the page button in front of the gates to open them up.

Okeydokey, Smokey!

While visiting Dave, I took the stethoscope from his room; I'm sure the nurses will look for it for a while. I took the briefcase to the bedroom and started to configure out the combination to open it. After about seven minutes, I opened it and found rows of money. But of course, I counted it the fast way and came up with fifty-two thousand dollars.

Jesus Christ, really? The cheap bastard thought that I would sell my country for fifty grand?

I was speechless for a while, but old school kicked in and I put my jaw back to close my mouth. Anyway, it was enough to pay for the plane and uniforms, so it kind of lightened my mood. I put the money in the safe and took the briefcase with me; I can get rid of it when we are in the air.

CHAPTER 37

They were all dressed as pilots, and I was dressed as a stewardess. Let me tell you, a stewardess's short skirt and high heels are very hot on me!

I rented a limo, and we all got in, including the still unconscious Yuri and his accomplisher. The driver was a little surprised to see two of the pilots out of the conches but did not say anything. I was in the front seat and was chitchatting with him all the way to the airport.

The way he looked at my legs and the drool that almost came out of his mouth were enough insurance for me that he was not going to mention or remember anybody else on that ride but a cute stewardess.

When we got to the airport, I got out of the car and pushed the button to open the gates. The operator asked me to show my ID, and after what seemed like an eternity, we heard a buzz, and the gates opened up. We drove in.

I thanked the driver and gave him a twenty-dollar tip. He was absolutely smitten with this chick!

Now we had to go through security and everything else to get to the plane. We also had to carry two "dead bodies" unnoticed somehow.

While I was giving my driver's license and passport for verification, I was flirty with the guy and making unscheduled looks at his package from time to time.

"A couple of our colleagues sort of overshot the runway last night." I smiled and perked my boobs up. "Do you mind if my crew puts them in the plane first?" I said and licked my finger. "Oh my goodness, I think I caught myself on something in my purse!" It was not too hard to play "a little girl" who got hurt.

Keeping the finger on my lips, I offered him my purse. "Can you please look in it, because something was sharp." I closed my eyes multiple times with that "innocent stupid girl" look.

According to my husband, stewardesses are "stupid." I looked like what a typical stewardess should look like . . . I thought.

He dumped everything from my purse on top of his desk and started looking at the various items, which you can typically find in the women's purses.

While he was getting my lighter with the pointy Russian Federation emblem on it, my crew got both Yuri and his bodyguard on a plane. *Hallelujah!* I thought in my head.

After he found the lighter, the officer told me that I was not supposed to take items like that on a flight, so I saucily said that he can keep it until our flight is back home.

"We will continue our discussion later!" I said and ran toward the airplane. "My name is Alex, by the way!" I yelled, almost at the plane.

CHAPTER 38

I flew on those high heels and up those airplane stairs like a butterfly.

First, I counted all my people. Everybody was inside the plane. Second, I noticed that our prisoners were starting to get back to the reality. It was a little faster than I had anticipated.

Never mind, I told the "pilot and copilots" to go and show their credentials to the guard before we could take off.

While they were outside, I set up the tanks and connected the masks to keep our guests from doing something stupid. Finally my guys came back, and we were cleared for takeoff.

In the air, I was contemplating with how to play Yuri's and his bodyguard's death without getting a conviction.

Because all of us were wearing the pilot uniforms and they looked like they are real things, I told my guys to put the parachutes on and prepare to abandon our ship.

We all did right in time to have our two prisoners put on the plane's front seats as a "pilot and copilot." With this done, I took the masks off and asked Shamoose to put the plane on autopilot mode till we almost reach the Cavendish beach.

As soon I saw the waters, I told everybody to jump. I took the ten gallons of laughing gas, and before I jumped, I shifted the lever to land.

I jumped in the army because it was a prerequisite to graduation, but let me tell you, what a feeling of jumping up from the perfectly good airplane!

We all landed in the closed area, and we all found each other in about thirty minutes.

I saw the plane diving into the waters of the sea. Holy crap, now it was finally over! But of course, we would have to see the news of the plane crash in Canada and have to make sure that there were no survivors.

We got back through the security and passport control in our regular clothes so as not to set up any red flags on both sides. All of us got back in one piece back to US, and now, driving home from the airport, I was thinking how to cover the airplane crash with no stewardess in it . . .

I think I just got it!

I changed back to my stewardess's uniform, came to the same gate to the private airport, and pushed the button to come in. After I talked to the guard and told him that the plane crashed but the pilots asked me to jump before it did, I had more "comforting words" that I couldn't handle. I cried a little for more sound effect, and he gave my lighter back.

I was exhausted and a little shaky, so I excused myself and told him that I was going home.

But of course, it was time to get back and continue the battle with my real-life "demon" parents, Dave, and the dog . . .

The End

www.ingramcontent.com/pod-product-compliance
Lightning Source LLC
LaVergne TN
LVHW091554060526
838200LV00036B/830